BOOK THREE

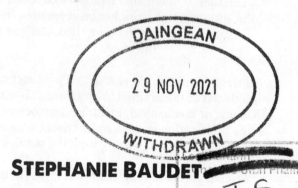

STEPHANIE BAUDET

Published by Sweet Cherry Publishing Limited
Unit E, Vulcan Business Complex
Vulcan Road
Leicester, LE5 3EB
United Kingdom

www.sweetcherrypublishing.com

First published in the UK in 2016
ISBN: 978-1-78226-267-1

Illustrations © Allied Artists
Illustrated by Illary Casasanta
Cover design by Andrew Davis

The Dinosaur Detectives: The Frozen Desert

Printed and bound by Thomson Press (India) Ltd.

CHAPTER ONE

'Wow!' Matt could hardly believe his eyes. The fossilised dinosaur egg that sat on the table in front of him was not big, but it was very smooth and oval, almost as though it was newly laid.

'It's a beauty, isn't it?' said his dad with a smile. 'I'm really curious to know what kind of dinosaur laid that.'

Matt's dad, Alan Sharp, was a palaeontologist – a very well-known one – and he was also a palaeo-artist. His paintings of dinosaurs and prehistoric life were sought after throughout the world. It was Matt's ambition to do the same one day, and he would be the third generation to do so because his grandfather had been a palaeo-artist too.

Matt picked up the egg and ran his fingers around the smooth, cool surface. It was shaped

just like a hen's egg, although a lot bigger and quite heavy. He closed his eyes and waited for his special gift to work.

He immediately felt the spinning, whirling sensation that was familiar to him now, although it became stronger each time he did it. It had begun when he was six; now he was twelve, and his dad relied on what Matt saw to make sure that his paintings were accurate.

The scene opened up in front of him. It was a forest, and several creatures stood in front of him nibbling small plants. These dinosaurs were small, only about sixty centimetres high, although their bodies and tails stretched out to about three metres.

They had large heads for their size, indicating large brains, and remarkably big eyes, making them look quite cute. Matt couldn't help but smile. They were really pleasant-looking, as dinosaurs went.

The grazing creatures were not aware of Matt's presence, since he wasn't really there at all, but now he found that he could turn his head a little and see what was on each side. It wasn't quite the same as doing it in real life, but remarkable, nevertheless. It seemed as though each time he did this visualisation, he became more part of the scene. Maybe one day, he mused, his ability would be available online to everyone.

The sun was low in the sky and he wondered whether it was rising or setting. The landscape didn't seem to have the tropical look that he'd seen previously while holding other dinosaur eggs. It seemed to feel cooler, and the vegetation was sparser.

For once it was a calm scene, with no predators lurking, so the cute little herbivores could graze in peace.

Back in the present, Matt looked at his dad and then described what he'd seen.

'Large eyes, you say? I think you were looking at a leaellynasaura. They developed large eyes

because they lived in Australia, but when it was much further south, inside the Antarctic circle. They needed large eyes to see during all those months of perpetual darkness.'

'It did kind of feel cold,' said Matt.

'Are you able to feel things there now, Matt?'

'No, not really, although I can look to either side now. It just had a cold look to it. I wonder if we will find any of those fossils in Antarctica.'

Now that Matt was twelve, he was allowed to go with his dad on fossil-hunting expeditions, as long as they were during school holidays. During the February half-term they were going to Antarctica to follow up some fossil finds and look for Mr Sharp's speciality – fossilised eggs.

CHAPTER TWO

Matt staggered a bit as he clambered ashore from the dinghy that had brought them from the ship, moored out in deeper waters. It was no wonder he hadn't got his 'land legs' yet, as they'd had a stormy trip through the Drake Passage from South America. That part of the ocean was notorious for its rough seas and they had been warned. In fact, it was reputed to be the roughest ocean crossing in the world.

Jo, standing beside him now and swaying a little, looked a bit pale. She'd been seasick for most of the two days. Her usually glossy black hair was dull and unkempt, sticking out from under her woolly hat.

Jo was Matt's cousin. It was becoming routine that she should come with them on the fossil-

hunting expeditions, although Matt was still not happy about it. For years he had looked forward to just being with Dad, but it seemed that Jo had nowhere else to go during the holidays while her parents, both doctors, worked hard.

'Feeling better?' he asked, trying to empathise with her. Matt was trying to be nice and say what was expected, mostly to please his dad, but he knew it must've been rubbish feeling ill for so long.

Jo took a deep breath, looked straight ahead of her, and then nodded. 'Much,' she said, letting out her breath in a white cloud.

It was cold, although not nearly as cold as Matt had expected. It was sunny, but with a brisk wind. And the scenery was stunning.

'Penguins!' Jo was pointing, colour coming back into her face. 'Oh look, Matt! Hundreds of them!'

The mass of penguins waddled towards them like a welcoming committee, but Jo and Matt soon realised that they were heading somewhere else, and almost ignoring the people clambering off the dinghy.

'I think they're Adélie penguins,' said Mr Sharp. 'Fortunately, they have had no reason to fear people.'

Jo went into raptures again and Matt rolled his

eyes, caught his dad looking, and had to smile. He had to admit that the penguins were cute and he really wanted to reach out and touch one, but they had been told not to.

'Just look at that!' It was his dad, now staring out over the sea packed with flat ice floes. Matt had to agree that it was breath-taking. Where there was open water, it was like a mirror, and so clear. Here and there in the expanse of sea, there were some enormous icebergs in an incredible blue, too. The flat white of the ice shelf glistened in front of them, stretching away towards higher ground and then the distant mountains. That was the direction they were heading, to Cassell Antarctic Research Base, located where the ice shelf met the land.

There was a Sno-Cat to meet them, bright orange and with four independent tractor-treads. The door opened and out jumped a cheerful-looking man with a broad smile. He almost ran towards them, hand outstretched.

'Alan Sharp,' said Matt's dad, shaking gloved hands. 'My son, Matt, and my niece, Jo.'

'I'm Ben Watson, base commander,' said the man, shaking hands with each of them. 'Where are the others?'

'Others?' said Mr Baker. 'There's only us.'

Ben Watson shook his head, looking beyond them. 'There are a couple of guys coming to make a TV documentary about bird migration. A naturalist and a cameraman. I thought you might have met up with them on board the ship.'

Mr Sharp shook his head. 'It was a rough crossing. No-one was feeling like socialising.'

'You climb into the cat out of the wind,' said Ben Watson, waving a hand behind him. 'I'll take care of your luggage and look for those guys.'

Excitement began to build up in Matt as he clambered aboard the Sno-Cat. It wasn't warm

inside, but it was out of the wind. He even exchanged a smile with Jo, whose dark eyes sparkled.

'Uncle Alan?' she said. 'I don't think Frank Hellman is going to catch up with us here, do you?'

Mr Baker smiled. 'On the remotest, coldest continent on earth? Hardly likely.'

But Matt wasn't too sure. Dad's rival, Frank Hellman, wasn't going to give up that easily. He meant business. He had already tried twice to steal the dinosaur eggs the minute his dad had unearthed them, and he'd almost got away with it.

Matt felt his dad's eyes on him. 'I can't understand why he's so determined to steal from you,' said Matt. 'Why doesn't he just go and find some fossils himself?'

'Oh, that's not Frank's way. He would rather let someone else do the work while he gets the credit,' said Mr Sharp. 'The rivalry goes back a long way. His father was awarded the Palaeontologist of the Decade instead of my father. Winning that award really launched his career. From being an outstanding scientist in the UK, he became world renowned overnight. I think he felt slightly guilty because he had discredited my father in order to win the award. When Frank and I were at University, Frank's father was our professor. He took a shine to me: we both got the same joy out of palaeontology. Frank, however, wasn't really interested and Mr Hellman senior was disappointed. When he died, Frank inherited his money, and he vowed to live up to his father's expectations, even though they had hated each other. I think Frank just saw how wealthy and famous palaeontology had made his father, and wanted that too.'

'So Frank is jealous of you because you had his father's friendship, as well as his help,' said Jo. 'He feels that he has to win the award.'

'Not only feels it. If you knew his father, you would almost feel sorry for Frank. He has to do it, and by any means. Both he and his father were beyond caring about ethics.'

The door opened then and two windswept men climbed in. Both looked bulky in their cold weather gear, but Matt could tell that the second man was big, although not particularly tall.

'Garrett Olson,' said the first one, pulling off his hood. 'And this is my cameraman ...'

He hesitated, and the other man said, 'Melvin Dyer.'

Garrett Olson grinned. 'Last minute change,' he said. 'My usual cameraman met with a slight accident.'

Mr Sharp smiled. 'How lucky that Mr Dyer was available at short notice.'

They settled down and Ben, the base commander, jumped into the driving seat. Soon they were on their way to the base, which would be their home for the next week.

CHAPTER THREE

Cassell Antarctic Research Base consisted of four wooden huts, connected by a corridor. One was the working area, one held the sleeping quarters, one the recreational area, including a well-equipped gym, and the fourth was the storage area.

Ben Watson gave them a tour round, and explained that in Antarctica, everything that was taken there had to be removed, and that included all waste. The motto was Leave No Trace. This beautiful, pristine land had to be preserved. It was the last unpolluted place on earth, although, of course, no-one could prevent airborne pollution, or the effects of pollution elsewhere in the world.

They each had separate tiny rooms. There were no luxuries, but they were warm and functional.

The one small window in each room had black-out curtains to help them sleep through the light nights.

Matt was surprised to find that there were about thirty people working at the base, though this dwindled to five during the long, dark winter months from April to October.

During dinner, they sat with the base commander and the two documentary makers.

The cameraman, Melvin Dyer, kept looking at Matt and Jo and finally said, 'I'm surprised that you brought your children, Mr Sharp. This is a tough environment with many dangers.'

Mr Sharp nodded, swallowed his mouthful,

and then said, 'They are both very interested. Matt wants to be a palaeontologist, too, so how better to learn about it than in the field?'

'You haven't come looking for UFOs, then?' said Garrett Olson, the naturalist. He grinned at Matt. 'There are lots of strange stories about extra-terrestrials …'

'Well, I've worked here for ten years and never seen any,' interrupted Ben, the base commander. 'You heard Mr Sharp. Matt and Jo are young scientists, not believers in fantasy.'

Matt had to admit, the subject did interest him, but he didn't want to seem as though he was contradicting Ben Watson or his dad. He had read about such things on the internet while researching in preparation for the trip.

Jo, however, had no such qualms. 'Why would they be here? I mean, it's just so cold and desolate.'

Matt sighed. Again, Jo had obviously done no research, otherwise she would know the stories already. He really didn't know why she bothered to come.

'The hollow earth theory,' went on Garrett, looking pleased to get an interested ear. 'Some people believe that the earth is hollow and that one of the entrances to the inner world is right here in Antarctica. They also believe that a race of super-intelligent extra-terrestrials lives in there.'

Jo's face lit up. Again, her dark eyes sparkled with interest.

'Nonsense!' said Ben. 'Anyone who knows anything about astronomy or geology would say that is completely ridiculous.'

Garrett shrugged, and Matt noticed that he winked at Jo.

It was an interesting theory, but, as Ben said, Matt was a scientist. He was not going to be drawn in to any far-fetched ideas like that, however plausible the arguments.

Matt couldn't help but think of the hollow earth theory, as he lay in bed that night. He had read about it and dismissed it as nonsense, but it was fascinating to imagine a world beneath their feet, where another race of people lived.

But it was crazy, of course! He should be thinking about the dinosaur eggs they hoped to find. Clear, proven science.

The next morning after breakfast, Ben Watson assembled them for the usual advice and warnings about the environment. Matt was used to this by now, having been on several expeditions to various parts of the world. He knew the importance of paying attention.

'I'll try not to make this into a lecture,' began

Ben, 'but there are some very important facts about being in Antarctica. There is no hospital here, just the base doctor, so do not take the weather or the terrain for granted. It might be a few degrees above freezing here near the coast in mid-summer, but this is the windiest continent on earth. The wind chill factor is very significant.

You all have your layers of clothing and I can see that you came prepared with the right gear. Keep it all on at all times. Frostbite can attack very quickly and the first symptoms are numbness and redness of fingers, toes, nose – any exposed parts.'

Matt felt Garrett's eyes on him and when he caught his eye, he winked. Ben noticed, and a fleeting frown passed over his face. He paused for a moment before continuing.

'The signs of hypothermia,' he said, 'are irrational behaviour, slurred speech and a feeling of being hot. The easy way to remember is: stumbles, mumbles, fumbles, grumbles. If that's not normal behaviour for you.' He gave a small smile.

'Finally, you bring nothing to this continent and you take nothing away, except, of course, that you, Mr Sharp, have permission to remove fossils after they have been carefully catalogued.'

He relaxed then, and really smiled. 'Oh, and one more thing … this is also one of the driest places on earth, a frozen desert, so make sure you are well hydrated. Drink plenty of water.'

The group dispersed, and Jo said, 'Are we going now, Uncle Alan?'

'No time to waste,' said Mr Baker. 'Ben is going to take us there in the Sno-Cat and then pick us up later. Get your outdoor gear on and let's get started.'

The site where the fossils had been found was at the base of an ice cliff. Ben explained that in the interior of the continent there were lakes thousands of metres under the ice, which were kept in liquid form by the heat of volcanic activity. The relatively warm water melted tunnels in the ice, and eventually flowed into the sea, washing down anything that was in the lake bed, like fossils of all kinds.

It wasn't far, and the three of them scrambled out of the Sno-Cat as Ben gave Dad directions down to the cave and handed him a satellite phone.

'There's a solar storm at the moment and it affects the signal, but it's not far back to the base and you can easily follow the Sno-Cat tracks, if you needed to.'

As the three of them watched Ben drive away, Matt felt a shiver of fear as he looked at the desolate but beautiful landscape stretching in every direction as far as the eye could see.

They were truly on their own.

CHAPTER FOUR

The climb down the ice cliff was tricky, but the slope was gradual, and the path was broken up into chopped-up ice. They all had crampons attached to their boots to reduce the chance of slipping. They were heading down to sea level, where a narrow shelf of ice bordered the sea.

When they were almost at the bottom, something made Matt turn to look back up the slope. He saw a dark figure watching them. Was it Ben? Why had he come back?

'Dad! There's someone up there, on the cliff!'

Mr Sharp and Jo stopped and looked back, but the figure was no longer there. 'It's easy to start imagining things here, Matt. It's such a strange place,' said his dad. 'Make sure you keep those sunglasses on at all times. The sun is strong, and the glare off the ice will damage your eyes.'

Matt had taken off his glasses, but now he put them back on. He was sure he had seen someone. A shiver ran down his spine. They were so isolated here, so vulnerable. But there were so few people, and all had their jobs to do, it was unlikely that any of Frank Hellman's men would be here. And they did have the satellite phone for use in emergencies.

But the excitement of the fossil hunt soon took all his attention as they entered the ice cave. It glistened pure white and blue, arching about five metres above their heads. At the far end, the roof sloped down a little but was still high enough for an adult to stand. Matt wasn't sure just how far in they would be going.

'It's beautiful!' Jo was in raptures again and this time Matt totally agreed with her. The three of them stared in awe. That turquoise blue was just stunning.

A small river flowed out and trickled down towards the sea, partially freezing as it was exposed to the cold wind. This was the river that Ben had spoken of, that came from a lake deep beneath the ice and carved its way down to the sea. Matt knew that Antarctica was a high continent, averaging 3000 metres above sea level. That's why the interior was the coldest place on earth. The ice sheet was up to 5000 metres thick. Five kilometres of ice!

They entered the cave, picking their way over the smooth ice, worn to a glassy surface by the river. Matt thought it was like being inside an enormous ice cube.

'Here's where the fossils were found.' Mr Sharp pointed to an area where the ice floor of the cave had been excavated.

'What kind of dinosaur was it, Uncle Alan?' asked Jo.

'It was a cryolophosaurus,' said Mr Sharp. 'Eight metres long and weighed a ton. We think that the males had a bright blue crest on their foreheads, and orange feathers.

'They lived about 160 million years ago,' said Matt, proving that he had done some research before coming. 'Early to mid-Jurassic period.'

Jo grinned, and poked him with her gloved finger. 'Show-off!'

Matt shook her hand away irritably.

'Right. We can't stand around getting hypothermia,' said Mr Sharp. He handed them each an ice pick. 'Let's make a start here on the wall of the cave near where the fossils were found. This isn't going to be easy.'

The ice was hard, but the picks were sharp. A lot of the ice was almost transparent so any fossils could be seen, but other sections were made of compacted snow so they were completely opaque.

They all worked hard. For one thing, it stopped them from getting too cold, and for another, there was nothing else to distract them. Matt remembered how different it had been in the Amazon rainforest. There were plenty of distractions there! Some of the wildlife, not to mention the illegal logging. Jo had really got worked up about that. Then in the Bahamas, there'd been the fire on board the boat – and the shark!

But here – nothing except the environment and the weather. The penguins certainly didn't pose any threat.

They had a break to eat a packed lunch, and then continued until four o'clock.

No amazing finds. Nothing at all. But that was fossil hunting: a lot of work but no guarantees of finding anything.

'Enough for one day,' said Mr Sharp. 'Ben will be here for us soon, and it might be trickier climbing back up that cliff than it was coming down.'

Out in the open again, they felt the wind cutting icily into any exposed skin and whipping up loose snow and ice particles, driving them into their faces.

They were just about to begin the climb up the cliff slope when Jo stopped. 'What's that?'

'What?' said Matt.

'A crying sound,' she said. 'Maybe a bird.'

'It's one of those aliens,' said Matt, laughing.

'Probably the wind,' said Mr Baker.

Jo frowned, her face only partly visible inside her coat hood.

Then they all heard it. A high-pitched plaintive sound.

'There!' Matt pointed. Further along the narrow ice shelf, something moved. 'What is it?'

They all crept forward, cautiously, not knowing what the creature was. It wasn't human, that was certain, and it wasn't alien either. It was black and white in colour.

'It's an albatross, I think,' said Mr Sharp. 'It must be injured.'

'It's huge!' said Jo.

'It has the biggest wingspan of all birds. Up to four metres.'

They kept their distance, not knowing what the bird might do. It looked at them, clacking its curved beak and trying to flap its wings, but one of them was obviously injured.

'Well, we can't move it, that's certain,' said Mr Sharp.

'Let's tell Ben,' said Matt.

By the time they reached the top of the ice cliff, Ben was there waiting for them in the Sno-Cat.

'Any luck?' he asked, his usual smiling face full of interest.

'No, but there's an injured albatross on the narrow ice shelf at the bottom of the cliff,' said Jo, bursting to tell the news first.

Ben's smile disappeared. 'Then we've got to save it before it dies of the cold. Those birds are scarce enough, and if it's out in the wind and unable to move, it won't last long. Come on, let's get back. We need something to carry it in, and it's going to take a few of us to lift it. Maybe Garrett and Melvin will help, too.'

Matt hoped so. He couldn't bear to think of that magnificent bird dying.

CHAPTER FIVE

The film team had just arrived back from their day's work, too. Melvin pulled off his woolly hat and shook out his thick curly hair. He eyed Matt and the other two.

'No fossils, then?'

'Not yet,' said Matt. 'Did you get some good film shots?'

It was Garrett who answered. 'Yes. A satisfying day's work.'

'Well, don't be too quick to take off your outdoor clothes,' said Ben. 'There's an injured albatross at the foot of the cliff and we need to get out there now if we're going to save it.'

'No time for a hot drink?' asked Melvyn, and Matt saw Jo frown at him.

Garrett started putting his hat and gloves back

on. 'No, there isn't,' he said. 'Do we know how long it's been there?' He looked at Mr Sharp, who shook his head.

'It wasn't there when we got to the cave this morning.'

Garrett gritted his teeth. 'I'll bet it's those long fishing nets again. I thought they'd been banned.'

There was no time to ask about that.

'Why don't you two stay here?' said Mr Baker, addressing Matt and Jo. 'I'm afraid you won't be much help so you might just as well warm yourselves up.'

'Oh no,' said Jo. 'I want to watch.'

Matt didn't even reply. He just pulled on his gloves.

Mr Sharp laughed. 'I guess the answer is no. Come on, then.'

Ben had picked up a strong net and they all piled back into the Sno-Cat.

'But you are waiting in the Sno-Cat,' said Mr Sharp, firmly, when they reached the spot. 'Promise you will not wander off anywhere or go near the cliff edge.'

They both nodded. 'We're not stupid, Dad,' mumbled Matt. He was sure his dad wouldn't have said that if Jo hadn't been there, but she could be impulsive if she was involved in one of her campaigns. This trip it was to be the plight of the albatross. He could see that already, and he had to admit that he shared her concern.

It was about twenty minutes before the men were back, their heads appearing first up the ice cliff path, and on their shoulders the huge bird, which they carried in a net.

Matt and Jo scrambled out of the Sno-Cat, eager to see the albatross close up. Its black and white feathers looked bedraggled and dirty, and the bird hardly seemed able to raise its head. It

was certainly not making any attempt to struggle and seemed content to let its human rescuers take care of it.

'I've never seen a bird so huge!' said Matt. He

was a little wary of the beak and stood back. He was sure that albatrosses were not vicious birds, but it must be very frightened.

Jo, however, reached out her hand, unable to resist touching it.

Ben shook his head. 'No touching the wildlife, please, Jo.'

They loaded it carefully onto the Sno-Cat and then all climbed back in.

'Do you think you'll be able to save it?' asked Matt.

Garrett shrugged. 'I'm a naturalist, not a vet,' he said. 'We can only do our best. Wretched fishing nets. That's probably how it got its injury. Some ships are still using long, baited hooked fishing nets which float on the surface. The birds come down for the bait and get caught and tangled in the nets.'

'Can't it be stopped?' Jo's outrage was simmering nicely and Matt smiled despite the situation.

Ben and Garrett both nodded. 'Many countries have already signed up to ban floating nets and to weight them so that they sink a little, but there are always those who prefer to ignore the ban, or even refuse to sign up to it,' said Garrett. 'Thousands of birds are killed every year, so these wandering albatrosses are now an endangered species. Imagine a magnificent bird like this becoming extinct.'

Back at the base, the bird was taken to one of the research labs. Someone found an old towel and placed it near a radiator in a quiet corner. Garrett volunteered to take care of it, fetched some drinking water, and got some fresh fish out of the freezer to thaw.

The next morning the albatross seemed to have improved a little, and Matt and Jo were allowed to see it.

'It's eaten some fish,' said Garrett. 'Always a good sign, I would think.'

The bird raised its head and looked at them with its frowning expression. It clacked its beak a couple of times. This time Jo did not try to touch it, but Matt wasn't sure whether it was because she'd been told not to, or because the bird's long, curved orange beak looked a little more threatening than it had the day before.

'Broken wing and a damaged foot,' said Garrett.

'So it's going to be a while before it's able to fly again,' said Matt.

Garrett nodded. 'I'll make sure that Ben lets you know when it's released. We'll be gone by then, too.'

The second day in the ice cave revealed

nothing, and Matt's enthusiasm began to wane. It was just so cold working in these conditions. He wasn't sure whether he preferred heat to cold.

He took a break just before they stopped for lunch, and wandered outside the ice cave, putting his sunglasses back on in the brilliant sunshine and dazzling ice.

A movement caught his eye, like someone or something darting out of sight.

Curious, and with memories of the stories of aliens and the hollow earth theory, he crept forward to where the ice cliff jutted out towards the sea. The small ice shelf narrowed here and Matt had visions of it breaking off and floating out into the ocean. He felt vulnerable on his own.

Then a figure stepped out in front of him. It wasn't an alien. It was Melvyn Dyer, the photographer.

Matt relaxed, although something in the man's face made him wary.

'Melvyn! I didn't know you were down here filming today.'

Melvyn ignored the question Matt was implying. 'Found any dinosaur eggs yet?' he said, smirking.

'Not yet,' said Matt.

'You're optimistic,' said Melvyn. 'Wild goose chase if you ask me.'

'We're used to it. But your journey here is worthwhile,' said Matt. 'Where's Garrett?'

'Looking after that stupid bird.'

'Matt?' It was his dad, calling from inside the cave.

Melvyn turned and picked his way as quickly as he could across the ice.

'Matt? Where are you?' Dad had come out onto the ice shelf, shading his eyes.

'Here, Dad. Melvyn was down here, trying not to be seen.'

'The photographer? Why?'

Matt shrugged. 'He wouldn't say.'

They paused for a moment, looking out to sea

at the flat floating ice and the reflection of the distant mountains in the mirror-like surface of the open water. Matt enjoyed in silence both the scenery and the feeling of being alone with his father, sharing this awe-inspiring place.

'Mum would love it here,' he said.

'Not the cold, she wouldn't,' said Dad, turning to smile at him. 'She hates the cold, you know that.'

Matt nodded. 'But she would love the desolation of the place, and the blue of the ice.'

'We must take some photos, Matt. Your mum and Beth will enjoy them.' Beth was Matt's younger sister.

Matt's few moments alone with his dad didn't last long.

'Hey! Where is everybody?' It was Jo.

'What's out there?'

'Nothing,' said Matt.

'Just Melvyn, for some reason,' said Mr Sharp.

Jo looked at Matt and frowned. Before she could say anything, Mr Sharp said: 'Come on, back to work. We can't give up on this fossil hunt, it has cost a lot of money to get us here.'

It was an hour later when Matt's ice pick broke through to another cave. It happened so suddenly that he almost slipped and lost his footing, despite the crampons.

'Dad!'

Mr Sharp's eyes widened as he peered through the small hole in the wall of the ice cave. He began to chip away at the surrounding ice, making the hole bigger. As soon as it was large enough to get through, Matt did so.

'Be careful,' warned his dad, 'the floor might not be stable.'

'Dad!' Matt exclaimed again. 'It's enormous!'

Soon the three of them were standing in a cave so huge that they could hardly see the roof, or the other end. It was bigger than an aircraft hangar, in fact, and Matt couldn't think of anything to compare it to.

Not only that, but in the clear ice floor, they could see what looked like a very large skull.

CHAPTER SIX

They spent the next hour carefully chipping away at the ice around the skull, gradually exposing it.

It was huge, about ninety centimetres long, and they could see many teeth. It was definitely a carnivore.

'What do you think it is, Uncle Alan?' asked Jo, leaning back on her heels for a rest.

Mr Baker nodded. 'I think it's a cryolophosaurus. They were about eight metres long and the males had a bright blue crest on their foreheads – or that's what is thought. We'll find out if we find any eggs and Matt can see one.' He pointed, 'But it looks like there's a lump here that could have been a crest. The females had a smaller, grey crest.

The males had orange feathers, too. Quite colourful for dinosaurs.'

They had almost dug the entire skull out of the ice. Mr Baker stood up to stretch his legs a little, and looked at his watch.

'Time to go. We'll have to continue this tomorrow.'

There was much to talk about back at the base and no reason not to reveal what they had found. It would have been impossible to hide their excitement. Even Mr Sharp could

hardly wait to tell everyone about the skull. He drew a quick sketch to give them an idea of what a cryolophosaurus looked like and they all crowded round, the excitement catching.

The albatross was improving, too, and Garrett and Melvyn had gone out to do some filming. They returned just before their evening meal was served, and were as interested as everyone else in the discovery of the skull.

'No eggs, though?' asked Melvyn.

'We've got a couple more days,' said Mr Baker,

'but the skull is a great find. It's completely intact, and don't forget, these fossils are not where they have lain for millions of years, they've been washed down by the melted water from the lakes.'

Matt looked at Melvyn. He seemed just a little too interested. And he had been a last minute replacement for the photographer who had an accident.

Melvyn caught Matt staring at him and he frowned. Matt smiled, not wanting the man to think he suspected him of being one of Frank Hellman's men. He thought he ought to warn his dad.

But he never got a chance. He was asleep by the time his father came up to bed and the next day proved very eventful for very different reasons.

By the time Ben drove them to the cave the next morning, Melvyn and Garrett had already left for their day's filming. They had heard about some snow petrels that had come ashore to breed, Ben told them, and were keen to study and film the beautiful white birds.

That will keep Melvyn busy, thought Matt, and relaxed a little. He would discuss his suspicions with Dad later.

The three of them freed the skull from the ice, and Mr Sharp held it up and turned it around gently for all to see.

Incredibly, it was intact, and Matt was amazed, as he always was, at the thought that it had lain there for millions of years and they were the first people to see and handle it.

Mr Sharp laid it gently at the side of the ice cave and they all stood up to stretch their legs.

Jo had wandered off a few metres further into the cave and suddenly she shouted.

'These might be eggs, or they might be just stones!'

Matt and his dad hurried over as fast as they could and looked where she was pointing.

Mr Sharp smiled broadly. 'Well done, Jo! I think you're right.'

Jo grinned at her Uncle, and then looked back at Matt as if to say 'I did it!'

Matt smiled back, if a little begrudgingly.

The eggs were easier to extract from the ice than the skull, because they were smoother and had a more regular shape. There were two of them, and they were round and about fifteen centimetres in diameter. In their fossilised state they were all joined together.

'I think it's time we had a lunch break,' said Mr Sharp, standing up again. 'We certainly deserve it.'

But as he stood up, he lost his balance on some uneven ice and toppled over backwards, hitting the floor with a thud.

'Dad!' Matt expected his father to groan a bit and clamber to his feet, rubbing bruised elbows and head, but he didn't move.

'He's unconscious!' Jo knelt down beside her uncle. Then she took charge. 'Matt! Where's the phone?'

Matt pulled it out of his dad's pack. He looked at it. 'No signal in here. I'll go outside.' But when he got outside there was still no signal and he reported back to Jo.

His dad still hadn't moved.

'You've got to go for help, Matt,' said Jo. 'Remember what Ben said. Follow the Sno-Cat tracks. I'll stay with Uncle Alan.'

Matt picked up his coat. 'Cover him with this, he'll get hypothermia lying there on the ice.'

Jo shook her head. 'Don't be daft! You'll get hypothermia. I'll cuddle up next to him to transfer some of my body heat. Hurry!'

Matt's heart was thudding and he felt sick with anxiety as he scrambled out of the cave again.

The weather had changed, too, and everything looked white. It was difficult to see the edge of the ice ledge and the sea beyond.

The wind was strong and blowing particles of ice in his face so that it felt as though he was being sand-blasted, and he battled against it towards where he thought the slope up the ice cliff was situated.

CHAPTER SEVEN

It was a white-out. Matt picked his way carefully along the ice ledge. There were lumps of ice where he didn't remember them before. The wind must be loosening parts of the cliff. Now and again the visibility cleared a little and he saw that the sea was very close, as if the ledge itself was diminishing. He knew that any moment it could break off and float out to sea to join all the other pieces of floating ice, but with him on it.

At last he found the slope up the cliff. That, too, was strewn with ice debris, but he mustn't fall. His dad was relying on him to get help. It was barely noon and Ben wouldn't be coming until four o'clock to pick them up.

He reached the top unexpectedly, and only knew he had done so because the ice under his

feet levelled out. The visibility was no better, yet he had to follow the Sno-Cat tracks. Matt peered at the ground but because there was no sun there were no shadows, just flat white.

He tried to orientate himself. He must remember where the ice cliff was. Was it on his right still? Suddenly, he was frozen to the spot with fear. One step could pitch him over the cliff and into the sea.

Then he felt a slight pressure on his gloved hand. It increased, and seemed to be pulling him forward, like someone holding his hand. Matt had no choice but to go. He thought of the extra-terrestrials, and even in his fear he managed a small smile.

Still he was being led. But was it towards danger or safety? He didn't know, but what he did know was that he had no choice. For one thing, whatever was impelling him forward was stronger than he was, and the other alternative was just to stand still while his father slowly sunk into hypothermia.

Then all at once, two things happened.

As the fog and snow cleared as the wind dropped a little he saw, right in front of him, Cassell Research Base, and the pressure on his hand disappeared. Matt looked round, but there was no-one in sight. Then he made for the base as fast as he could.

Ben and the other workers were astounded. 'How on earth did you find your way back, Matt?' said Ben. 'It's clear here, now, but only in the last few minutes. Wasn't the phone working?'

Matt shook his head. 'Dad's hurt,' he said. 'He fell and banged his head and he was unconscious when I left. Jo's with him. She said she would cuddle up close to transfer her body heat.'

Ben nodded and rounded up a couple of the workers as well as phoning the base doctor. He looked out of the window. 'It's clearing more, now. Let's go!' Then he turned to Matt. 'Any more discoveries?'

'Well, yes. We did find two dinosaur eggs. We had just dug them out of the ice when Dad fell.'

Ben smiled. 'Good,' he said, pulling on his jacket and gloves. 'Let's go.'

Again, Matt stayed in the Sno-Cat, and was relieved when he saw the men returning, dragging his dad on a long sledge. Dad was conscious now, and even managed a smile and a wave to Matt.

'I'm fine, Matt,' he said as they loaded him aboard the Sno-Cat. 'I was only knocked out for a minute or two, but I've sprained my ankle. Nothing serious, it's not broken, the doctor says.'

Matt was surprised that the dinosaur skull and eggs had also been rescued. Ben saw him looking at them.

'That lower ice shelf is breaking up, which is going to make it more tricky to get to the cave,' he said. 'Also, your dad's not going to be fit for any more fossil hunting on this trip.'

Back at the base, Matt and Jo watched as the doctor strapped up his dad's ankle and gave him some pain killers.

'Thanks for staying with Dad,' said Matt as he and Jo left Mr Sharp to rest, and they went to the recreation area.

Jo smiled. 'I think you had the difficult job,' she said. 'We didn't know there was a white-out outside. How did you find your way back?'

Matt was tempted to share his experience with someone, but not Jo. Not yet. He just shrugged. 'No big deal,' he said.

'Well, at least your dad has got his fossilised eggs – what we came for.'

Matt nodded. 'Where are they? Do you know?' He sat up and looked round as if expecting them to appear on the coffee table.

'They were brought in,' said Jo. 'But it doesn't matter, does it? They're safe.' She looked at him. 'Or do you have some suspicions?' Her dark eyes gleamed.

'Well, nothing much, but that Melvyn was hanging about and watching us, and he was a last minute replacement cameraman for the one who had an accident. You know how sneaky Frank Hellman can be…'

'We'll watch him without being too obvious,' said Jo. 'Let's go and see how the albatross is getting on.' She stood up. 'I wonder if there's anything we can do about that long fishing net thing.'

'Are you on a mission, again? Like the illegal loggers in the Amazon rainforest?' He raised his eyebrows.

Jo stopped and turned to look at him. 'Everything is so unfair!' she said.

CHAPTER EIGHT

The albatross was looking perkier and its white body feathers were pristine. It seemed to be putting a little weight on its injured foot, but the wing, of course, would take some time to mend.

Garrett and Melvyn had returned from their filming and heard all about Mr Sharp's accident. Garrett had brought some fresh fish for the bird.

'Albatrosses spend much of their lives flying,' he said, 'so their wings have to be strong. They only go ashore to mate and lay their eggs, and then they fly hundreds of miles in search of food for their young.'

The albatross clacked its beak as if to agree with what Garrett was saying.

After that, they went to see how his dad was, and also to find the dinosaur skull and eggs. Matt was anxious to hold the eggs and confirm that they belonged to the cryolophosaurus, whose skull they had found. He wanted to go into his vision state.

When he asked Ben, the base commander shrugged. 'I haven't seen them. Ask one of the men who brought them in.'

But no-one knew where they were. They seemed to have disappeared. Matt even asked Melvyn.

The photographer laughed. 'You're asking me? Why would I have your fossils? Aren't you leaving tomorrow, too? I'm off to pack.'

'I wonder if that includes the fossils,' said Jo. 'They'll take up a lot of room and be heavy, too.'

'He has a lot of equipment bags. I'm sure he'll find space.'

Mr Sharp was well enough to enjoy his evening meal with everyone else. It was their final meal on the base, too, so the permanent staff were eager to make the most of their visitors.

Although Matt and Jo watched Melvyn, he wasn't in a hurry to move from the table, and later he and Garrett went to play cards with some of the other men. He was still there when Matt and Jo went to bed. He must have hidden those fossils somewhere. Dad hadn't asked about them, probably assuming that they were all ready to take with them. Funny he didn't seem anxious for Matt to verify the dinosaur. He obviously hadn't recovered properly yet. Matt was glad, though. He didn't want to worry Dad about the eggs yet.

But as Matt was pulling his blackout curtains, he saw a movement outside, where, of course, the sun was still shining, although low in the sky.

A hooded figure was disappearing round the side of one of the huts. It was impossible to see who it was because everyone looked the same in their outdoor clothes, with their faces hidden by fur-lined hoods and sunglasses.

Matt grabbed his jacket and gloves and ran for the door. As he passed Jo's room, she emerged, also pushing her arms into her jacket sleeves.

'I saw him, too,' was all she said.

The wind hit them in an icy blast as they stepped outside. It seemed much colder with the sun lower in the sky. Matt pointed round a corner of the building and Jo nodded, both leaning forward into the wind.

They saw him then, pulling something heavy from where he'd buried it in the snow near one of the huts, and stuffing it into a bag. Although he couldn't possible have heard them, he looked up at that moment before they had time to duck out of sight.

He dropped the bag and the fossils and, in one swift motion, he grabbed them both by the arm and dragged them towards the Sno-Cat. Before they had time to struggle, he had pushed them in, shut the door, and driven off at speed, bumping over the uneven ice.

But just as he had closed the door, Matt saw his face.

'Ben!' he whispered.

Matt was stunned. It wasn't Melvyn after all. It was Ben, the station commander, who was on Frank Hellman's payroll.

'Ben?' said Jo, beside him.

'Yes! It's Ben, not Melvyn.'

'I can't believe it,' she said. 'He seemed so nice.'

After about ten minutes the Sno-Cat stopped. They peered out and could just see the shape of a small building.

The door opened. 'Out!' shouted Ben above the noise of the wind.

Matt looked round. It was just flat white as far as he could see. He thought about running but knew he wouldn't get far, and what about Jo?

Ben opened the door of the hut and pushed them inside. 'Meddling kids!' he said. 'I'll let you out tomorrow after the ship has sailed with my cargo on board. And don't try to escape. This area is covered with crevasses and some of them will be covered with snow now, which won't hold your weight. You'll step on it and ...' He pointed downwards indicating their fall into the abyss. Then he slammed the door shut and Matt heard him turn a key.

It had been some sort of supply store, Matt guessed, but was now abandoned and empty except for a couple of wooden crates. They sat down on them. There was one small window letting in a tiny bit of midnight sun so that he could just see Jo's silhouette.

'We can't just sit here,' she said. 'We'll miss our ship, Uncle Alan will be worried to death, and ...'

Matt interrupted her. 'Frank Hellman will have won.'

Jo nodded.

'But you heard him, Jo. The place is covered with hidden crevasses.'

'He says,' said Jo.

'Are you willing to call his bluff?'

She shrugged and looked round. 'If we had a big stick we could prod the snow in front of us before taking a step.'

'And how long would that take? That's assuming we know the way back, which I don't. We'd freeze to death.'

'Anyway, there's no stick,' said Jo. 'And this isn't the sort of place we are likely to find one lying about.'

'We could follow the Sno-Cat tracks, except that with that wind, they'll be covered already,' he said. It did look as though they would have to wait to be released. But what happened if they weren't? No-one would ever find them here.

It was cold but at least they were out of the wind. They lay down on the floor next to each other trying to keep warm. Common sense overcame Matt's normal aversion to cuddling up to girls. Body heat was the only thing between them and a long, cold night.

But Matt couldn't sleep and he suspected that Jo was still awake, too. After an hour or so he got up, trying not to disturb Jo in case she was sleeping. He went over to the window and looked out.

'Jo!' He wanted her awake now.

'What?' She got up and came over to the window. There was no irritation in her voice at having been disturbed. 'What is it, Matt?'

'Look!'

'Penguins,' she said. 'Yes, Matt, there are a lot of them in Antarctica. Millions, in fact.'

'Yes, I know, Jo, but do you think penguins know where the crevasses are? Do you think they can sense them?'

Jo was quiet for a moment. 'Animals are usually good at that kind of thing,' she said, looking out at the flock they could see not far from the hut. 'But these are smaller and lighter than us.'

'I know. What did Dad call them? Adélie penguins? But don't you think if we were amongst them we'd be safe?'

Jo looked at him in the dim light. 'Yes, but we still don't know our way back to the base.'

'That's true, but I can't just sit here. We have to try. And I remember that on the way here the sun was behind us.'

Jo went to the door and rattled it. 'We're locked in, remember.'

Mat picked up one of the crates. 'Stand back,' he said, and heaved it at the window, which shattered completely. 'Now we're not,' he said, grinning. 'If Ben thought we would just stay here like good little kids, he was wrong.'

'Like sensible kids,' said Jo, for once being the cautious one.

Matt knew it was rash to try to find their way back, but he ignored the little voice of common sense inside his head.

He squeezed through the small window and was soon standing outside with Jo beside him.

CHAPTER NINE

Matt realised that there was no going back. The hut would be freezing cold now with the window broken, and they had made their decision, even though he knew it was probably not a sensible one. He could hear his father's voice in his head telling him to await rescue, that missing the ship didn't matter as long as they were safe, that losing the fossils to Frank Hellman didn't matter, either.

But Matt was determined, and he could see that Jo was, too. She was certainly not one to hold back.

The penguins were not moving much, they were asleep, Matt thought. They had young with them, although not chicks. These were about half the size of the adults. Between them and the penguins there was a distance of about a hundred metres.

They began carefully, aware that with each step they could pitch into a crevasse.

'I wish we had a rope,' said Matt. 'Then at least we could rope ourselves together.'

They held hands and took it in turns to lead, pushing at the snow in front of them, testing its firmness. It was a slow progress. Matt hoped the penguins wouldn't move away.

Jo took a turn at leading. They were getting used to the process now and their pace had quickened. Suddenly, as Jo pushed her forward foot into the snow and put pressure on it, it gave way. She screamed, and pitched forward, the snow beneath her feet falling away into the hole that had appeared in front of them.

Matt felt the sudden tug on his hand and his reflexes made him tighten his hold, but gloved hands are not secure, they slip easily and, as Jo dangled in space over the crevasse, he could feel his fingers slipping.

'Matt! Save me!' she screamed, trying with her other hand to grasp the lip of the crevasse, her legs swinging wildly in an effort to find a foothold on the sheer edge.

Matt took off his other glove with his teeth and, kneeling in the snow, he grasped her other hand and pulled.

Jo's face was white with fear as she struggled for her life. Somehow, she found the strength to dig her boot into the side of the icy crevasse wall and push herself up and over the rim. As soon as she was on safe ground, she flopped onto the snow, her shoulders heaving with breathlessness and, Matt thought, tears. And he didn't blame her. He almost felt like crying himself.

This was crazy. They'd become a bit complacent and she could easily have slid down into that seemingly bottomless split in the ice. The horror of it almost made Matt turn back, but it was Jo who recovered first.

'We'll have to see how long the crevasse is, Matt,' she said, getting to her feet. 'We've got to go round.'

Matt just nodded and put his glove back on. His fingers were beginning to tingle a little.

It took an hour to reach the penguins. Matt looked at his watch. Three o'clock. The penguins ignored them except for moving to one side as Matt and Jo walked into the flock.

Matt looked into the sun, just above the horizon. 'The way back has to be towards the sun,' he said. 'It hasn't moved much since Ben brought us here.' He pointed. 'There's a high place over there. We might be able to see the base from the top.'

The flock of penguins was vast and stretched as far as the higher area Matt had seen, so it didn't take them long to reach it. They didn't know for sure, but had confidence in the penguins knowing the safe ground.

The wind had increased again and bit viciously at the bare skin on their faces and made it difficult to breathe. The hand that Matt had exposed still felt tingly, and he was worried about frost-bite.

From the high ground they could not see the base, maybe because the visibility was poor, or maybe because it just wasn't in that direction.

Matt felt a pang of fear. They should have waited in the hut and trusted Ben to let them out as he had said. At least they wouldn't have frozen to death. Now they were out in this vast white wilderness and it could take any rescuers hours to find them. Hours in which they could have frozen to death.

Jo walked close to him and she was shaking, whether with cold or still with shock at her narrow escape, Matt didn't know. With no base in sight, they silently continued to walk towards the sun, which was now beginning to rise higher in the sky.

As the sun rose, the haziness began to clear, and suddenly they could see the huddle of linked huts about five hundred metres away. They looked at each other and grinned, but it was short-lived as Matt realised that there were no penguins in that five hundred metres.

Was it because they didn't want to be there, or because they knew something – that the ground was unstable? All at once, the small distance seemed like miles.

As they watched, a figure came out of one of the huts. He was carrying a box.

'Help!' Matt shouted. The figure stopped and turned just as Jo hissed, 'It's Ben!'

They both flung themselves onto the snow and Matt wished his jacket wasn't such a bright red, but that was the point, of course. What had he done?! He'd acted without thinking, in his relief at seeing someone. The one person they didn't want to see. All this would be for nothing, including Jo nearly falling down a crevasse.

They didn't dare move, they hardly dared breathe as Ben continued to look in their direction. Then he seemed to shrug and turned back to continue towards the Sno-Cat. Matt and Jo stayed where they were. Maybe he was going to come and investigate in the Cat.

After loading his box containing, Matt guessed, the fossils, Ben jumped into the driving seat and

started up the motor. With relief, they watched as he drove away in the opposite direction. Then they slowly got to their feet and brushed off the snow.

When someone else emerged from a hut they knew it was all right, and both yelled as loudly as they could.

It was a relief to reach the base again, and to sit down in a comfortable chair and drink hot chocolate. But not before they had alerted Mr Sharp about Ben.

Mr Sharp shook his head. 'I can hardly believe it, he seemed such a nice guy.'

It was still early and Matt and Jo had not been

missed yet. They quickly packed their bags, and one of the other workers offered to drive them to the ship in another Sno-Cat. Matt had the doctor check his hand and was relieved to learn that no permanent damage had been done. They had managed to contact the ship's captain by satellite phone and Ben was already handcuffed when they arrived there, and awaiting being handed over to the Argentinian authorities.

When he saw them he gave a derisive laugh.

'You may have lost this one, Sharp, but remember that wherever you are, we won't be far behind. Frank's got plenty of other interests.' He looked at Jo. 'Remember that pile of logs you found yourself adrift on, in the Amazon rainforest? They were his logs, floating all the way down the river into his bank account.' He laughed again.

Jo looked at Matt and he could see her fury boiling up beneath the surface. However bad they had thought Frank Hellman was before, now he seemed even worse.

CHAPTER TEN

The crossing back through the Drake Passage was relatively calm, and Matt finally had a chance to hold the dinosaur eggs.

They were in their small cabin and his dad watched as he closed his eyes and the vision swam into view and settled into focus.

In front of him a cryolophosaurus, with its bright blue crest and orange feathers on its forehead, stood eating the corpse of a small animal. He heard something and raised his head, staring to Matt's left. Matt looked round. Another dinosaur stood there, one that Matt couldn't immediately identify. It was slightly larger than the cryolo, and was eyeing the carcass hungrily.

In an instant it charged; the cryolo stood

his ground but was whipped by the other dinosaur's immense tail. Matt imagined he roared, although he didn't have the ability to hear things yet. The other dino was round and charging again, this time knocking the cryolo to the ground. Now he was at a real disadvantage as the dino stomped on his chest.

The cryolo got to his feet surprisingly quickly and took the offensive. He had had enough of the food thief. He charged, buffeting into the dino with great force and knocking him to the ground this time. He seemed winded or even injured and the cryolo sensed that he wouldn't have any more trouble from this one and went back to eating. The dino struggled to its feet and limped away into the forest.

'Wow!' said Matt, coming back to the present. 'What a fight, but the cryolophosaurus won.'

His dad nodded. 'And did he have a blue crest and orange feathers on his head?'

'Bright orange,' said Matt, and his dad smiled, picked up his pencil, and began to sketch. 'And Dad, I could feel the ground under my feet and the wind in my face that time.'

Two weeks after arriving home Matt and Jo received an email from someone at Cassell

Antarctic Research base. There were two pieces
of news. The first was that a new commander
had arrived to replace Ben. The second was that
the albatross had been released that morning,
fit and well.